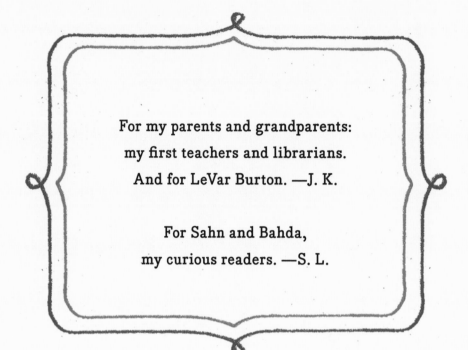

For my parents and grandparents:
my first teachers and librarians.
And for LeVar Burton. —J. K.

For Sahn and Bahda,
my curious readers. —S. L.

Library of Congress Cataloging-in-Publication Data

Klausmeier, Jesse.
Open this little book / by Jesse Klausmeier ; illustrated by Suzy Lee.
p. cm.
Summary: Die-cut pages open to reveal different animals, each opening a book of a different color and
reading about the next.
ISBN 978-0-8118-6783-2 (alk. paper)
1. Books and reading—Juvenile fiction. 2. Colors—Juvenile fiction. 3. Animals—Juvenile fiction. 4. Toy and
movable books—Specimens. 5. Board books. 6. Books and reading—Fiction. [1. Colors—Fiction.
2. Animals—Fiction. 3. Toy and movable books. 4. Board books.] I. Lee, Suzy, 1974– ill. II. Title.

PZ7.K678214Ope 2013
[E]—dc23

2012002129

Design by Sara Gillingham Studio.
Typeset in Bodoni Egyptian.
The illustrations in this book were rendered in pencil and watercolor
and were digitally manipulated.

Manufactured in China.

3 5 7 9 10 8 6 4 2

Chronicle Books LLC
680 Second Street, San Francisco, California 94107

www.chroniclekids.com

OPEN
THIS
LITTLE
BOOK

by Jesse Klausmeier · illustrated by Suzy Lee

chronicle books · san francisco

Open this . . .

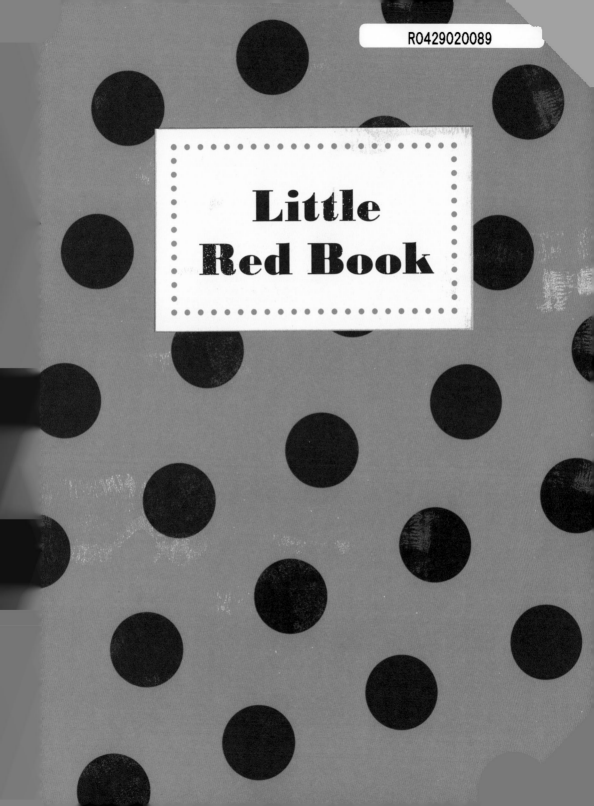

Little
Red Book

and read about Ladybug,

who opens a . . .

LITTLE GREEN BOOK

and reads
about Frog,

who opens a . . .

Ladybug closes her
little green book . . .

You close this
little red book . . . .

and . . .

open another!

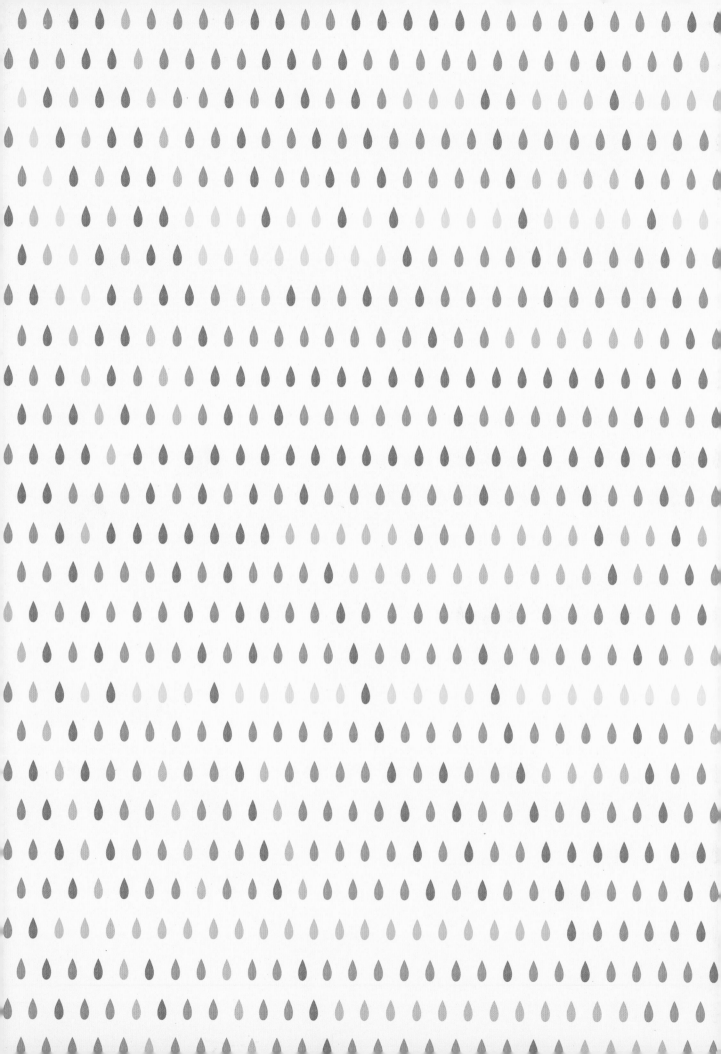